Molly Mischief

My Perfect Pet

DEAN

Originally published in Great Britain 2017 by Pavilion Children's Books
This edition published 2023 by Dean, part of Farshore
An imprint of HarperCollins*Publishers*
1 London Bridge Street, London SE1 9GF
www.farshore.co.uk

HarperCollins*Publishers*
Macken House, 39/40 Mayor Street Upper,
Dublin 1, D01 C9W8, Ireland

Text and illustrations © Adam Hargreaves 2017
The moral rights of Adam Hargreaves have been asserted.

ISBN 978 0 0086 1743 1
Printed in China
001

A CIP catalogue record for this title is available from the British Library.

Stay safe online. Farshore is not responsible for content hosted by third parties.

This book is produced from independently certified FSC™ paper
to ensure responsible forest management.

For more information visit: www.harpercollins.co.uk/green

Molly Mischief

My Perfect Pet

Adam Hargreaves

Hello, my name is **Molly**.
Sometimes people call me **Molly Mischief**.

I have **lots** of ideas.
I think they are very good ideas, but not everyone agrees.
I know my mum and dad don't agree when they shout
my name **very** loudly... that happens quite a lot.

MOLLY!

Today my dad took me and
my brother to the zoo.

We saw lots of different animals.
My brother liked the monkeys best
of all. They are **nearly** as ugly as he is.

I got into trouble at the zoo.

Molly!

Don't pull faces at the warthog!

Molly!

Don't chase the parrot!

Molly!
Don't wake up the flamingo!

Molly! Don't tickle the penguin!

ice cream

Molly!

Don't feed the crocodile!

And then I found a hippopotamus.
It was very big.

Much bigger than my pet mouse, Polka.
She is tiny.

I wish I had a big pet.
A big pet like a hippo.

I took the hippo home.

But my mum and dad weren't very happy about my new pet.
I had to take the hippo back to the zoo.

If I can't have a hippo,
then I wonder what other pet I could have...

I like bears. How about a big bear?

There was a polar bear at the zoo.

I took the polar bear home.

But polar bears like the cold and my bedroom was too hot.
And I don't think a polar bear would fit in the fridge.

I had to take the polar bear back to the zoo.

**Then I found a giraffe – the tallest animal in the world.
I took the giraffe home.**

But the giraffe would not fit in my bedroom. I had to cut a hole in the roof. Dad was not very happy about that.

Molly!

I had to take the giraffe back to the zoo.

My family are very hard to please.

I had to take the tiger back to the zoo.

And the rhino.

And the walrus.

And the big bird.

And the big snake.

I want a big pet
A large pet.
A giant pet.
A huge pet.

And then I found just
what I was looking for.

An elephant!

Now, that would be
a big pet.

So I took it home.

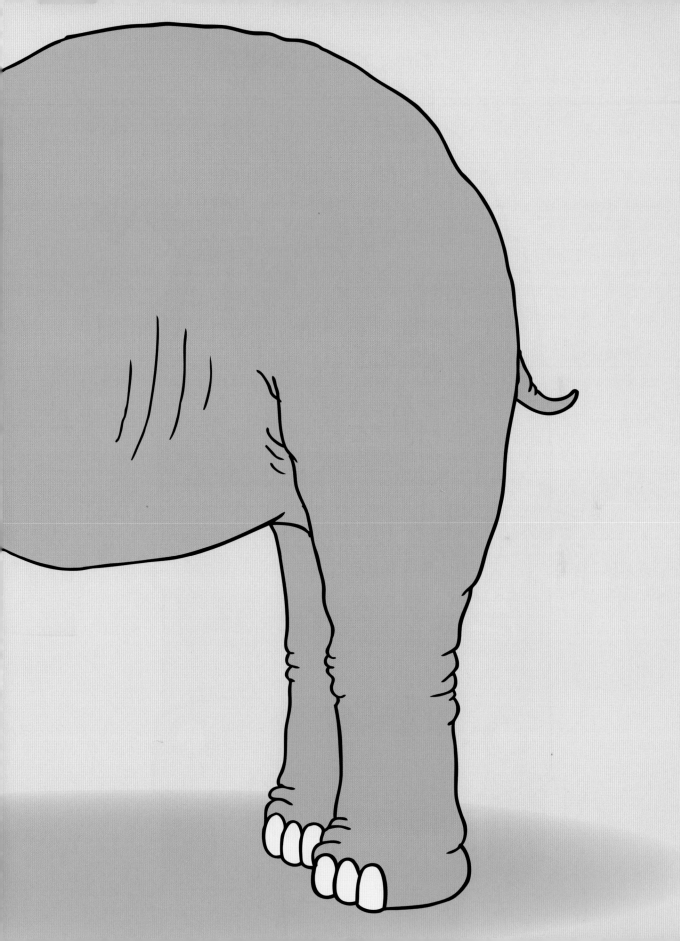

On the bus!

It was fun playing with my elephant in the garden.

It was great fun taking my elephant for a walk in the park.

It was brilliant fun taking my elephant to show and tell at school.

It was giggly fun tickling my elephant's tummy.

And it was messy fun building a kennel for my elephant.

But then my elephant got me into trouble. It ate our neighbour's garden.

And my elephant was **not** house trained.

And my elephant squashed our car.

Molly!

I decided that maybe a pet elephant was not such a good idea after all.

So I took my elephant back to the zoo.

When I got home, Polka was waiting for me. Then
I realised something. I already have the **perfect** pet; the
perfect-sized pet. A pet that doesn't get me into trouble.
Which just goes to show, bigger is **not** always better.

Although there are some things
that are better when they are bigger.
Like...

Surprises!